I0734432

A bitter wind assumes the shape of a trumpet

A bitter wind assumes the shape of a trumpet

copyright © 2016, *4ink7*

ISBN: 978-1-943661-04-6

A bitter wind assumes the shape of a trumpet is Issue Two of *4ink7*, a literary journal that is a book. Individually, all rights revert to the authors upon publication. The title is taken from Ted Pearson's "The Markov Chain."

No part of this book may be copied, transcribed, or distributed except for quotes in promotional or educational formats.

Printed in the USA

4ink7
PO BOX 4945
Chattanooga, TN 37405

Editor: Russell Helms
Associate Editor: Hannah Sandoval

Cover and text design: 47 Journals

Contents

Emily Dickinson
Renunciation — I
XX. — 3
XVIII. Apotheosis — 4
Troubled about Many Things — 5
XXXVII. — 6

Amy Gerstler
*How Happy I Was When Mother Bought Me
    Those Three Dresses* — 7
Translation — 8
A Tour of the Late Composer's Home — 11

Adam Vines
The Apostle — 12
Tristesse I: Mattress as Canvas — 13
Tristesse II: Manifest Destiny, Late 20th Century — 14
Cortical Arousal — 15
Re-Stroke II — 16

Ted Pearson
from The Markov Chain — 17

T. Crunk
Daybreak — 24

Hank Lazer
N27P46 — 27
N27P67 — 28

Robert Carr
The Holiday Poem — 29

Linda Frost
For Sale — 30

Paul Naylor
from Luminous Ruse — 33

Rowan Johnson
   Bucharest   38
   Budapest   39

John Stupp
   At Smalls Jazz Club   40

Lori Lasseter Hamilton
   Facebook Post: I'm Glad that You Have Kids   41
   Facebook Post: It's My Birthday!   43
   Facebook Post: Vacation Pay Check   46

J.R. Solonche
   I Am Tired of Owning Things   50

Contributors   53

Emily Dickinson

Renunciation

from a facsimile of the same poem within *Poems,* 1901

There came a day - at Summer's full -
Entirely for me -
I thought that such were for the Saints -
Where Resurrections - be -

The sun - as common - went abroad -
The flowers - accustomed - blew,
As if no soul - that solstice passed -
Which maketh all things - new -

The time was scarce profaned - by speech -
The falling of a word
Was needless - as at Sacrament -
The <u>Wardrobe</u> - of our Lord!

Each was to each - the sealed church -
Permitted to commune - <u>this</u> time -
Lest we too awkward show
At Supper of "the Lamb."

The hours slid fast - as hours will -
Clutched tight - by greedy hands -
So - faces on two Decks look back -
Bound to <u>opposing</u> lands.

And so, when all the time had leaked,
Without external sound,
Each bound the other's Crucifix -
We gave no other bond -

Sufficient troth - that we shall <u>rise</u>,
Deposed - at length the Grave -
To that new marriage -
<u>Justified</u> - through Calvaries - of Love!

Emily Dickinson

XX.

(from *Poems, 1901,* "First Series—Life" Gutenberg electronic
edition)

I taste a liquor never brewed,
From tankards scooped in pearl;
Not all the vats upon the Rhine
Yield such an alcohol!

Inebriate of air am I,
And debauchee of dew,
Reeling, through endless summer days,
From inns of molten blue.

When landlords turn the drunken bee
Out of the foxglove's door,
When butterflies renounce their drams,
I shall but drink the more!

Till seraphs swing their snowy hats,
And saints to windows run,
To see the little tippler
Leaning against the sun!

Emily Dickinson

XVIII. Apotheosis

(from *Poems,* 1901, "First Series—Love" Gutenberg electronic edition)

Come slowly, Eden!
Lips unused to thee,
Bashful, sip thy jasmines,
As the fainting bee,

Reaching late his flower,
Round her chamber hums,
Counts his nectars -- enters,
And is lost in balms!

Emily Dickinson

Troubled about Many Things

(from *Poems,* 1901, "First Series—Time and Eternity"
Gutenberg electronic edition)

How many times these low feet staggered,
Only the soldered mouth can tell;
Try! can you stir the awful rivet?
Try! can you lift the hasps of steel?

Stroke the cool forehead, hot so often,
Lift, if you can, the listless hair;
Handle the adamantine fingers
Never a thimble more shall wear.

Buzz the dull flies on the chamber window;
Brave shines the sun through the freckled pane;
Fearless the cobweb swings from the ceiling --
Indolent housewife, in daisies lain!

Emily Dickinson

XXXVII.

(from *Poems,* 1901, "First Series—Time and Eternity"
Gutenberg electronic edition)

If I shouldn't be alive
When the robins come,
Give the one in red cravat
A memorial crumb.

If I couldn't thank you,
Being just asleep,
You will know I'm trying
With my granite lip!

Amy Gerstler

How Happy I Was When Mother Bought Me Those Three Dresses

They don't make dresses like that anymore. Not like when I was
a girl, in Europe. Hand-stitched, lined with silk. High waisted or
drapey. Moiré, rose, and midnight blue. I'd give anything to see
those dresses again. To rub my fingers across the little embroidered
jackets we wore over them. We emigrated so young, my cousin and
I, all by ourselves. She hit it big in Hollywood during the forties.
When her first movie opened at Cannes, you wouldn't believe
the limousine traffic. After the war, visiting Vienna with my new
husband, I pretended I didn't know what the old man in the bath-
ing cap shouted in German. Shriveled and paunchy, towel tucked
around his waist, he pointed at me and yelled: "Get out of the pool,
Jew, you're polluting the water!" Two attendants rushed up and
suggested he leave, tugging his arms, but he planted his feet on the
tile and kept yelling. I floated easily on the water's surface, while,
quoting the new laws, they removed him. When I climbed out of
the pool everyone stared. I was wet and golden-haired, young and
pretty back then, taking my time drying myself. The other swim-
mers stood in the shallow end, silent. I never went back to that
swim club. Every December in America, my children had a Christmas tree. One bank account I keep hidden, in case I need to disappear. Am I, in ways I can't see, unclean? Who is this trapped in
me, Jonah imprisoned in his whale, a small girl on an ocean liner,
refusing to speak, surrounded by people who don't know German,
hands clapped over her ears? Tonight I'll pick my way down the
cliff where my pretty home sits, to the ocean's foamy lip. As I soak
the torn garments of my body, I'll pray: May the waves fade these
stains.

Amy Gerstler

Translation

a rising stroke   a falling stroke
a crooked form   a hooked stroke

this quickly inked character means
one who's sexually ambidextrous

what some claim are characters
taken from the Chinese
others believe to be lifted
from the secret language of women

those Sanskrit words are giant cauldrons
they contain so much simmering history

the words and phrases "loves," "anticipates," "longs for," "believes,"
"seizes," "bedazzled," and variations of such words and expressions
will not be considered
as binding or having any mutually agreed upon meaning at all

or maybe it was just more untranslated
terrorist chatter?

individual words and letters
become extinct all the time
no one uses that consonant anymore
so drop it before you humiliate yourself

a secret language
only women could read
what did these females
write to each other
when they thought they were alone?
what stories were handed down?

The Girl Who Saved a Fort
Sojourner Truth's Youth
Joan of Arc Taken Prisoner
Lady Godiva Apocrypha
The Tomboy Who Tamed a Nation

The Land And Our Language Before White Men Came:
What Was It Like?
This Book Is Filled With Such Enthralling Knowledge

this verb means *to travel for the purpose of improving one's health*
this noun means *a present brought back from a perilous journey*

she feels like one of a series of hesitantly drawn characters
vibrating almost imperceptibly on the page, with meanings like:
a grain afloat on the ocean
go ahead, nibble away like a silkworm or engulf like a whale, I'm ready to be ingested
the root cause of all our woes

the Chinese word *lin* has a range of meanings
not exhausted by any single word of another language

this dictionary is arranged according to the number of strokes
required to draw the characters
those with fewest strokes coming first

The man who found America
(though it was never lost
according to those living there at the time)
The man who invaded America
communicated with the natives by signs

these colloquialisms adopted in recent years
by the elite—a bunch of thieves, grease monkeys

and brawlers, who nonetheless
set themselves up as our rulers
and banned our native tongue—

this character means *a man allergic to kindness*
these two characters mean *the mouthpiece of a hookah*

here we have a quiescent vowel,
shy as a kid on her first day of school

the dazzling anger of men has its own language
the jagged language of the jilted
insects hum vegetal intention
wood nymphs burble
     as they dance, draped in rain,
in a language whose alphabet's composed
of little images of trees

the alphabet is my tribe
and I mean to live quietly among them
bending my body into meaningful shapes
perhaps entwined with yours
using our whole persons to confess
what can't be, by any other means,
comprehended or expressed

Amy Gerstler

A Tour of the Late Composer's Home

"Here's the room where he wrote his funeral music.
He was headed for the boneyard, but you didn't hear him
grousing about it. Ardor characterizes his funeral
tunes, dedicated to the woods he loved, dripping with
winter." (She walks to the baby grand, plinks out
a tune, sings: *Is this how you vanish, dear planet?*
Silent, submerged, as coral rebuilds its polyps and colonies?)
"Look, here, on the piano," she says, "preserved
all these years, his funeral march, intended only
for himself, the sheet music shoved under his last
glass of milk, like a napkin, to blot spills."

Adam Vines

The Apostle

Picasso's *Woman Playing with a Small Cat*

To lure it
from her finger
curls, she rips out

a tuft, dangles it
like a liver

lollipop—the cat
now at a lap revival

strikes a midair
hallelujah.

Adam Vines

Tristesse I: Mattress as Canvas

Philip Guston's *Couple in Bed*

Always the soles
of work boots
and a table

of broken ankles,
soles cut
at the heel

like a leaner
cocked on a post—
another toss

shy of a ringer—
and even
in bed: sapling

tibias, soled
but unmanned,
resting on the top sheet

like mauls, Guston's
and his wife's heads
conjoined, bulging

like a single brain, but still
he squeezes the brush handles,
horsehair petalled,

angry with paint,
thumb cocked, hitching
a ride to his next canvas.

Adam Vines

Tristesse II: Manifest Destiny, Late 20th Century

Frank Moore's *Prairie*

Of course
snow falls
in the bedroom:

ice crystals
like raised bites.

Buffalos
the size
of bedbugs

migrate across
the comforter,

their violet
trailings
the only proof

that they
were really there.

Adam Vines

Cortical Arousal

Picasso's *Acrobat*

Discharge leg,
one hand

en pointe,
the other

a dislocated
fork. Sniff

own butt. Go
to the café:

bend backward
to impress!

Adam Vines

Re-Stroke II

Artschwager's *In the Driver's Seat*

The pointy man next to me
says, "Ah, to be
that skinny!" And I say,

"Yes, we are plump!" "Speak
for yourself," he responds

and skinnies off to *Door II*.
And I wonder if I should have said,
"and, ah, to be that naked!"

So I name the naked guy
on the beach pretending

to be in the cockpit
of a dragster *Skinny*
and the pointy man *Cock*.

Ted Pearson

from *The Markov Chain*

1.

Early autumn blueprints a new theogony.

Transcendental wasps build nests of pure duration.

Neighborly aporia serve topical drinks.

The streets are abuzz with seasonal aperçus.

2.

The years between siestas were spent on belay.

Deadbeat demons learn the lyrics of damnation.

A hard rock face and its gritty murmurations.

Precisely as dreamt, wounds anticipate their scars.

3.

Systems theory often leads to misspelled trouble.

Consciousness housebreaks granulated meanings.

Scandalous objects speak with a westbound twang.

The reticular formation is our first best hope.

4.

A bitter wind assumes the shape of a trumpet.

I would trade some rack time for a bright patch of noise.

As the sky in the window grows dark on the page,

Ghostly musickers arrive, long of tooth, and sage.

5.

A tincture of terror deracinates graphemes

Whose kennings testify to thought's conclusive *thunk.*

Fear lays in wait for the perfect subject. Don't sweat

The *punctum* – or try to affect the sublime.

6.

Trauma blooms nightly in a darkened theater

Where magic beasts forage for unspeakable dreams.

A paradox favors an irresolute cause.

The logical city is not where you would think.

7.

Few centaurs survived the narrative that followed

Their fateful encounter with the old fabulist.

The tang of dead flowers tweaks distant memories.

In arkestral majesty, the Sun God departs.

T. Crunk

Daybreak

Comes the last
hour of night
as we sleep—

blue moon
sails back into her harbor
of white clouds

fireflies
night watchmen
snuff their lamps
make their way home

the snails
steadfast guardians
lay down their armor
and rest from their patrol.

Then
first light—

crickets
rise in chorus
strum harps and zithers
a morning
hymn to the sun.

Beetles
emerge from their grottoes
in dark cowls
reciting morning prayers.

At the edge of the harvest field
grasshoppers
sharpen their scythes
waiting
for the white
mist to lift.

Beneath pavilions
of gilded leaves
caterpillars
weave and spin
their regal tapestries

and butterflies
unfold their rich
embroidered robes.

Great caravans
of black ants
embark on expeditions
to undiscovered worlds.

Brigades
of goldclad wasps
return to building
their holy cities
raising high
its parchment temples

and spiders
hoist their fretwork bridges
vaulting
spire to spire.

Troupes
of gypsy gnats
rehearse their aerial ballet.

Dragonflies
in winged chariots
set out across the pond

as legions of locusts
din from the bank—
Pha-raoh
Pha-raoh
Pha-raoh

and retinues
of water striders
perform their daily miracle.

Then
we wake

to daybreak

the world beginning

rise
as morning rises

greet the dawning
as it passes

grateful

for this day
of small things.

(from *To His Son,* a chapbook to be published in 2016 by
GreencupBooks)

Hank Lazer

N27P46

3/7/14

each sense

„The morning possession of a body brings
in the face of the horror of the disease of forgetting
with it

its power of changing levels
and changing pitches." ‹262›

as the possession of a voice brings with it

the possession of a voice brings with it

early morning   namu amida budsu

begin again

nonetheless beginning

the power of changing levels

a set of structured breaths   meditation   a

whose acquired results it uses; my personal existence must be

the taking up of a pre-personal tradition." ‹265›

the sequel to a pre-history

a turn by daily deliberation   a

end of understanding, space, just as

counting slides into accounting   &   a

„my history must be the

door way into necessary self
forgetting

the morning precious again

Hank Lazer

N27P67

4/10/14
diamond head

here what do you say does not also increase
within this flow of words when across to
whether one's distance from them own more

Robert Carr

The Holiday Poem

I read my poetry at the holiday table
but this year was told explicitly, *Don't.*
This year, Dad brought his own poem
by his favorite author, Mary Oliver.

So my father convenes my court
and opens *Blue Horses.* He reads
about yoga, being unable
to touch toes as Mary turns
into a lotus.

My sister breathes
for the first time in ten years,
This is the best Christmas ever!

It seems not everyone
enjoys tears at the table
or the blood of dead mothers
in their cranberry sauce.

I decide to forgive myself:
*"Let the soft animal of my body
love what it loves"*,
and curl up on the couch.

Linda Frost

For Sale

White Cape-Cod style two-story home with 3 bedrooms, 2 ½ baths, *large living room with adjoining dining room and a bay window that overlooks the pastoral sloping backyard. The main level boasts an additional family living area with working wood fireplace, bonus bedroom or study, and a separate laundry/utility room. The downstairs includes a half-finished family room with significant space for storage on the other half.*

This is a must-see property, not only because of the plethora of living space and fine maple floors, but because the owners feel you really must see it. According to them, like a certain glass slipper, it's looking for its true owners. Mind you, there is nothing wrong with the house; it is rather the current owners who have never fully appreciated its possibility.

Take the husband, for instance. When he fights his way out of another dead sleep, avoiding the day's despair before the sunlight can sneak its way onto his face or legs, the first thing he notices is not the striking green of the oak's leaves that bend their way toward him from the bedroom window. It's not the breeze that brushes his forehead as he works to sit up and take notice. No. He sees only the bird shit from the robin that hourly hurls itself into the window screen for no apparent reason. It's not the meadow of which Thomas Jefferson would have been proud that catches his eye when he stumbles to the bathroom and looks out onto the backyard. No. It's the 1.6 acres that will need mowed before it rains that registers for him. It's the 1.6 acres that will need cut again in just days that he sees as he leans one hand on the mildewed shower door to sigh and pee.

The wife's another story. Her dissatisfaction has to do with a suspicion born the day they closed on the house. As the lawyer drew up the final documents, the seller produced a forgotten sheet of paper disclosing a hidden story of mold in the basement. Since that moment—one swiftly brushed off; the sellers had taken care of it; surely all was well?—whenever she stepped onto the basement stairs, she sniffed and imagined and worried. And—although no one would ever actually voice it—she often wondered what—or who—else might be living in the house with them. Her oldest said she'd seen people in old-fashioned clothes walking through her closet on their way to the crawlspace behind, and the youngest was afraid every night of some scary someone making their way into her room. The house seemed to the wife to be never quite theirs, never quite within their grasp.

We firmly believe the house to be a fine home for someone. After all, the fireplace invites, particularly those swallows that make their impossible nests just inches above the stack of unlit firewood. The mouse village must be right under the kitchen sink although the cats seem to believe it lies somewhere closer to the refrigerator. Even the garage welcomes; while the outdoor tabby sleeps in luxury on a lamp-lit pillow, skunks waddle back and forth across the concrete floor.

Yes, we know the house will suit its next owner beautifully. The backyard with the storm-tossed trampoline and spray-painted picnic table—"Lucy ★" says one side and the other, "CORA ❤"—should host gathering after gathering, should glow each summer night from the embers in the fire pit down by the stand of cedars. The creek should be overrun with toy cups and teapots and the garden plants, ever heavy with tomatoes. The spare rooms were often full in this house, but perhaps the right owner will need them for their mother, their father, their home-wanting friend. Perhaps the house with these owners was never quite full enough.

So: as the cigar smoke lifts from the study, the litter box is scooped for its final stinky time, and the washer halts its last walk across the tile, we encourage, we implore, we pray for the next

owners—the *right* owners—to come forward, pay down, lay claim.
Please, we beg, let us go home; yours is right here.

Paul Naylor

from *Luminous Ruse*

To sit with the question of what kind

of being asks what it means to be
the kind of being who asks   what words

alone can ask   what it means to ply
a raft of words against the current's surge
and cross over   as metaphor does   from here

to there   a leap logic fails to make
where *A* both is and is *not A*.

Which sutra says what it means to write?

~

What anyone heard   who heard?   Slow rising mountains

groan and travail under pressure from below   ignis
intrudes on the world hovering above   who heard?

A voice excluded   excluding itself   as they rose
from below   when no one was   to hear
the middle voice in early tertiary   when no

one was   to watch the Wasatch Mountains rise –
even its echo suspect as the imagined sound

of the sea in retreat one final time.

~

This gadarene life capital calls for yet can't

quite contain   a brazen belief in this triage
of middle-class cares the hedge fund priced in.

Who casts their eyes on the debt ceiling
above   a prayer to nothing at its best –
an avowal of form fallen on hard times?

This malaise of greed defines the age she
must find her way in   the prey awaits

word from the top   all options signed off.

~

For a few minutes each morning   set aside

all these tired stories I tell of myself.
Drop the adjectives first   then adverbs   then nouns –

leave only *is* to follow the path breath
takes against the bustle I've become   an endless
clash of chatter about what I thought was

but isn't to be.   Breathe cool air in
warm air out.   *Is* will find its way

along a spine aligned with this story's end.

~

Mine is a mind far too busy thinking

about being rather than being   isn't as I
thought   the guileless way cirrus clouds can drift

across the sky   higher than mind   no hurry
to reach their point of dissipation   my eye
too restless to follow their slow approach   gathering

against the horizon   no storm holding them back
the blue they breathe into the vast no

eye can see   too busy to know it.

~

Such odd angles she takes toward the source

I am surprised by   daily   her world begins
as an oblique repeal of what came before –

the doll of last month's love   no longer
an object of attention   Jessie   forgotten by Emily
again   shoved under a bed   dead to desire.

Four and a half years into this wonder
the sparkling pink wand she conjures me with

the play imagination makes   the alembic of change.

~

The sublime is being eaten by bark beetles

in mountain standard time   ponderosa and lodgepole pine
are dying from New Mexico to British Columbia

the rust color of death among still living
green   awaits an infestation killing from the inside
out   larvae eat the sweet cambium that feeds

the trees.   Winters don't get cold enough anymore
to kill bark beetles thrive in endless droughts

brought on by a who or a what?

~

Between *is* and *is not*   Buddha's middle way –

taken as an antidote to belief in either
apart from the other   imagines each as empty

of essence   as nothing but an opening for
the other's taking place   in the blank space
between *is* and *is not*   the middle voice –

its timbre an imagined essence   asks if what's
between is beyond or is what's beyond between?

Is there a buddha who wouldn't answer yes?

~

'Do I contradict myself?   Very well then   I

contradict myself'   since I become in a culture
that   by the bond of commodity and capital

breeds me   a living contradiction   unable to step
back from that fact   except here   between lines
of a lyric   dark strife lights a rift

where awareness might seep in of the *skandalon* –
of that trap snapped shut.   What might let

that light   led by reflection's bias   sift in?

~

Rowan Johnson

Bucharest

In downtown Bucharest, a short stroll down Calea Victoriei from Nicolae Ceauşescu's balcony in Revolution Square leads to the garish National Military Museum with the imposing Intercontinental Hotel towering overhead. While the sky may not always be grey, it seems to fit the landscape. When wandering among the ruins, heavy rain and cloudy skies provide a perfect atmosphere and there is no desire for the weather to change.

The range of small avenues around the museum offer something of an architectural salad, dominated by Neo-Romanian structures, Transylvanian Gothic cathedrals, Moldavian churches, functionalist office buildings as well as staid dormitory-style housing blocks. Each building is interspersed so that there is no theme to the place; rather it seems like a mismatched display of Ceauşescu's grandiose visions mixed in with the stark reality of centuries' worth of poor central planning. The buses, too, can sometimes be loud, hurtling machines with leaky roofs and very questionable electric wiring. And then, sometimes the buses are clean and air-conditioned and run smoother than a Toyota Prius.

At times, Bucharest seems like a grey and desolate city on the verge of imploding under the weight of its crumbling ruins and abandoned buildings. But by waiting a few minutes and turning a few street corners, Bucharest soon becomes just another modern European city, waiting with characteristically open arms for rich tourists.

Rowan Johnson

Budapest

His soul stretched tight across the skies that fade behind a city
block... what would the man who wrote the Preludes think of this
place? By 4am the buses already thunder along Rakoczi Street.
Industrial-strength sirens blare through the early morning haze of
Budapest. Soon, taxis and scooters whine along the road too. From
Budapest's Keleti Train Station, it is a short walk to the Danube,
but a dangerous one.

This Hungary, poor and downtrodden, barely gripping onto the
edges of Europe like a falcon's claw. Over the Danube itself, the liberty statue soars over the piles of trash scattered all the way down
Kiraly Street as the ruinpubs crumble into the bleariness of day.
The bottles of vodka and rum elongate the bars in the cool light.
Tables and chairs scatter across the room in elaborate shapes.
From the psychedelic shisha of Szimpla Kert, all the way to the Keleti, tourists stumble back to their hotels. In the dark corner, a man
with a harmonica breaks his tune to say a simple "hello" while the
tourists scurry into their locked buildings. A cavalcade of falling
clocks and ticking clocks erupts. The night simmers slowly away.

John Stupp

At Smalls Jazz Club

Ralph
Lalama
from
Aliquippa
can't see
cats
crawling
on the bar
at Smalls
to whom
everything
has to be
explained
by horns
until
they forget
to sleep
like rubbery
sailors
their eyes
won't close
over
deep water
until
someone
turns the
music off
with a biscuit
at the end

Lori Lasseter Hamilton

Facebook Post: I'm Glad that *You* Have Kids

Hmm. You know, I never know what to say when people at work
ask me if me and my husband have any kids. It's a little hard to
explain why a couple who has been married for 10 years doesn't
have any kids. I mean, I got asked this week at work if me and my
husband have any kids, and I just said "no." No one asked me why
but I felt the need to explain why for some reason, but I didn't.
I mean, it's kind of like when people ask how you're doing. The
socially acceptable response is, "Fine, thanks." No one really wants
to hear how you are really doing. Your husband just got diagnosed
with diabetes, his brother keeps blowing up his phone to ask for
money, you don't know how you're gonna pay the power bill this
month because your husband lost a lot of hours at work from when
he was in the hospital and all the doctor's appointments he had to
go to, etc. I mean, who really wants to hear my life story when they
simply ask me how am I doing. So when people ask me if I have
any kids, I just say "no." I refrain from saying that I was diagnosed
with breast cancer at age 34, and then I developed a blood clot in
my heart from my chemotherapy port, and I had to take Coumadin
for the blood clot, and Coumadin causes birth defects, and I didn't
get married till I was 34 so about the time most people start having
kids after they get married, well, that choice was out for me unless
I wanted to have a kid with birth defects. And then last year I had
to get a hysterectomy because I had a uterine fibroid that got so big
that the fibroid tissue started dying inside my uterus and the dead
tissue started coming out of my vagina. So I don't have a womb
anymore. I could tell people all that to make them feel sorry for
me, make them think I wanted kids but couldn't have any because
of all my medical issues. Poor, tragic me. Or I could tell them the
truth and say I never really wanted kids. I have always been afraid
that my husband and I are too poor to afford them. We only have a
one-bedroom apartment, and I am selfish at heart and don't want
to have to sacrifice going to poetry slams and open mic poetry
readings whenever I want to, in order to stay at home and take care

of a child. How do you deal with feeling like a cultural anomaly, a "freak," for being married and being a woman and never having any kids and not wanting any? I just wish that people would stop asking me if I have kids because it makes me feel like a freak and makes me go into a deep self-examination that I didn't really want to get into in the first place.

Lori Lasseter Hamilton

Facebook Post: It's *My* Birthday!

i am upset. why does my own mother treat me like i am less than, unworthy, not as good as her or anyone else? last week she came over and asked me where i want to go out to eat for my birthday. i said "either Little Donkey or Cheesecake Factory." i work until 6:30 pm, so i wouldn't be able to get to a restaurant until 7:30. well, she said, "if we go to the Cheesecake Factory we might have to wait, there is always a crowd there." i said in response, "the thing is, they have good desserts that i like." then she said, "we'll see." i want to know why she asked me where i want to go to dinner for my birthday if she was just going to shoot me down. it is my birthday, don't ask me where i want to go for dinner if you don't really want to go certain places. why did you even bother asking me?! why did she have to say, "we'll see" like i was a 5 year old screaming kid in a grocery store pestering her to buy me a candy bar and throwing a temper tantrum?! you asked me where i wanted to have my birthday dinner, don't ask me if you don't really care! i am sorry if it is inconvenient for you to go to the Cheesecake Factory at 7:30 at night and maybe wait till 8:30 to eat, but it is MY birthday! i can't help the fact that i don't get off work until 6:30! ugh! she makes me so mad! why does she have to say, "we'll see" so coldly in response. if you don't really want to go where i want to go for dinner, do me a favor and don't ask in the first place. why did you ask to begin with—to pretend to care, because you feel obligated to take me to dinner because i'm your daughter? next time, do me a favor and don't bother if you are going to treat me so coldly and like i am unworthy and less than. i am 42 years old and i make my own money, i can take myself out for my own birthday, thank you very much! i am not going to be limited in where i can go out to dinner for MY OWN DAMN birthday!

every time i talk with my mother in person or over the phone here lately, she is either trying to control me, tell me what to do, or make me feel less than. i mean, i don't think my own mother realizes how special i am. i won the poetry slam last weekend! i competed against 6 other poets and won, and let me tell you the other 6 poets were no amateurs! all but one of them were slam veterans and very talented! how is my own mother going to treat me like a speck of dust and say, "we'll see" when i tell her i'd like to go to dinner for MY birthday, when she asked in the first place?! don't ask if you don't really care. i hate it when people ask me what's wrong and they interrupt me when i am telling them what's wrong or if they ask me what i want for my birthday and then they shoot me down or are critical of the restaurant i mention or the gifts i say i would like. i am like, what's the point of you asking me in the first place if you are going to interrupt me, shoot me down, criticize me, etc. because you REALLY DON'T CARE to begin with and you are just asking for appearance's sake?!

ever since i found out that my parents are letting my sister stay in the townhome they bought until their house sells and they didn't tell me (i found this out from my sister), i feel hurt and betrayed. why are my parents hiding things from me? they never offered to help me and robbie get a house, condo, or townhome. we have to pay rent on our apartment. why are they helping my sister and not me? on top of that, why did they hide that from me? i feel like my parents are trying to exclude me from their lives, estrange me, make me feel like i don't belong, make me feel like a second-class citizen. i found out a few weeks ago about the townhome issue. i was already feeling excluded and left out and hurt by my family before my mom came over last week and asked me about my birthday. but when she said, "we'll see" when i mentioned the Cheesecake Factory as one of my choices for a restaurant, that really was the last straw. i am tired of dealing with her. she either likes to have power over other people and be in control of everything, even other people's BIRTHDAYS, or she likes to make me feel inferior. or a combination of both. you know what, i don't want to be around her if she is going to treat me like that. i can take my own damn self out for my birthday, thank you very much. don't treat me like a second-class citizen on my birthday. i deserve to be treated better than that. and not just simply because i am your biological daughter (unless there is something i don't know, like maybe i am adopted). also because i am special. i don't think my own parents realize

the fact that God loves me enough to bless me with winning the
poetry slam, which i haven't won in 16 years. He loved me enough
to bestow His favor on me to the point where i won a slam with 6
other very talented poets. i am really tired of my mother treating
me like i don't belong, hiding things from me, and acting like her,
dad, and my sister are the only true members of the family and that
i don't deserve to belong to their little club. well, you know what
i say to that? exclude me and i'll exclude you. maybe robbie and i
will just disappear right after i get off work on thursday and take
off to the restaurant of my choice without telling anyone and maybe i will turn off my cell phone. how about them apples?

Lori Lasseter Hamilton

Facebook Post: Vacation Pay Check

i have been having a sort of existential crisis the past couple of
weeks or maybe the past month or maybe the past two years, i
don't know. but here lately things have sort of come to a head and i
have been feeling very sad and alone. i feel like i have to apologize
for my very existence here lately. maybe i shouldn't be saying all
this, but here goes. i am deeply wounded by the way certain people
have treated me/are treating me. one of them is my supervisor on
my temporary assignment. sometimes when i go to his desk to ask
him a question, he rubs his eyes and/or tells me to wait and holds
his index finger out to indicate to me that i need to wait. i feel like
he is irritated by me and thinks i am stupid and gets irritated when
i ask him a question. being on a temporary assignment, not being
able to find a permanent job in the 2 years since i was laid off is
bad enough—it makes me feel like there is something wrong with
me. but on top of that, to have my supervisor act irritated when i
ask a question, makes me feel even worse about myself. i feel stupid for asking questions but i want to make sure i get the job done
right. i feel like i should apologize to him for asking him so many
questions and irritating him. it makes me feel bad about myself
when i see him rubbing his eyes when i ask him a question.
the other person who has really wounded me a lot lately is my
mother. last year, i got a vacation pay check from my temp agency
when i reached my one-year anniversary date of being with the
temp agency, which was july 20th. i told her last year about the vacation pay check i received, and i wish i hadn't. this year, a couple
of weeks ago, before july 20th even came around, she called me
one day and barely said hello before she asked, "did you get your
vacation pay yet?" honestly i felt like i was being manhandled by a
loan shark used by the mafia. i hadn't even told her that i might get
my vacation pay this year. well, here's the thing—let me tell you
that for the past year, she has been paying one of my bills every
month—she pays my alabama telco loan monthly payment of $120,
every month, because i cannot afford to pay it. since i was laid off

from my permanent job in 2010, i have made less and less money.
my first temp assignment, i made $11 an hour. now, on my second
temp assignment, i am only making $10 an hour. it is a struggle for
me to be able to pay all my bills. she wanted me to pay her $120
back this month for the alabama telco loan payment she made,
since i had extra money. i guess that's fair and reasonable. however, to me, if a parent knows their child only gets extra money once
a year from their job, they shouldn't demand part of that money.
to me, the parent should want their child to be able to enjoy that
money. well, i was planning on buying some new clothes and a new
bedspread with my vacation pay money. my bedspread has a stain
on it that won't come out. i have washed it several times, and it
won't come out. it looks like a grey pencil mark or ink mark. i have
been wanting to buy a new Simply Shabby Chic bed set for a really
long time, and finally, i thought, here was my opportunity to do so.
well, i was wrong. i gave my mother a check for $120 on monday.
then, after giving her my check, she had the nerve to ask me what
i was going to do with the rest of my money. she told me i should
either save it or pay some bills with it. it's bad enough that she
took part of my money, then she has the nerve to tell me what to
do with the rest of it! i wanted to stand up to her and tell her, look,
it's bad enough you took part of my vacation pay money, you have
no right to tell me what to do with the rest of it! after all, I earned
that money—i am the one who has been going to work every single day and getting to work on time every single day for the past 2
years for the same temp agency, not her! i have to get up at THREE
THIRTY in the morning every day to be at work at FIVE AM at
my current assignment! I am the one who has been making those
sacrifices, not her! how dare she tell me how to spend the rest of
my money! i got $300 vacation pay, and $120 is almost half of it!
what the hell can you do with $180?! for some reason, i am afraid
to stand up to my mother. i am 42 years old and she is still trying
to control me, she thinks she has a right to tell me what to do. i
am so tired of her. my own parent wanting to take my vacation pay
money has deeply wounded me. it really hurt my feelings the way
she asked, "did you get your vacation pay money yet?" over the
phone. she asked that question in a very demanding tone of voice.
between her taking my extra money i only get once a year, telling
me what to do with the rest of my money, and my supervisor mak-

ing me feel stupid, i have begun to question my own existence. in other words, if people find it so easy to mistreat me, should i even exist? people make me feel bad just for existing by the way they treat me—particularly my mother and my supervisor. i have been afraid to express my feelings because my feelings are ugly. honestly, i am full of hatred and resentment toward my mother, and i have been stuck lately as far as being able to write any poems. i feel like if i cannot honestly express myself, i shouldn't bother writing poetry. if i cannot be truthful or honest in my poetry, why bother writing at all. so i haven't written any poems in a while. that really makes me angry that people have made me feel so bad about myself and the feelings that i have that it has made me stop writing poetry. i feel like other people have been in total control of my life lately. i used to be such a rebel. where has my courage gone? i want to put a stop to other people controlling me especially if it means i stop writing poetry. no one has a right to put me through that kind of existential crisis. i used to be the type of poet that said "motherfucker" as part of a poem on a microphone at City Stages spoken word festival, but i don't know where that girl has gone now. i think she has disappeared forever. and i don't like it one bit at all. i guess i am afraid if i write a mean, hateful poem about my mother, if she or my sister or another family member ever comes to a poetry reading, i will hurt their feelings. why i should care about hurting my mother's feelings, i don't know. she has damaged mine. it has been 11 years since i lived at home, and i don't get any help financially from my parents other than my mother paying that alabama telco payment every month. she does pay my health insurance too, but I DID NOT ASK HER to do that. when i got laid off from my permanent job in 2010 through no fault of my own because the company i worked for closed, i lost my health insurance. she signed me up for the state of Alabama's health insurance plan. but i did not ask her to pay my health insurance. the only bill i have asked her to pay is the alabama telco bill. i guess she thinks she has a right to control me, tell me what to do with my life, and treat me any way she wants just because she is paying that bill for me. believe me, if i could pay that bill myself, i would. if i ever get a pay raise, i will start paying that bill in the hopes that she will have less control over me. but i have a feeling that even if i did start paying that bill, she would still try to control me.

i was asked to be a featured poet at a Sister City Connection poetry
reading this past Sunday night, July 29th, and for a month i strug-
gled with what to write. the theme was transformation, and to me,
my ugly feelings of hatred and resentment and feeling unworthy
of existing did not translate to being able to write a positive poem
about transformation. because of the way other people have been
treating me, i was terrified for a month that i wouldn't be able to
come up with a poem for the reading. to me, it is an honor to be
asked to be a featured poet for a reading. i am really angry that i
had to go through that kind of struggle with writer's block because
of the way other people have been treating me. no one should
make me feel like that.

J.R. Solonche

I Am Tired of Owning Things

I am tired of owning things.
I am tired of having.
I am tired of owning a house which I have to heat in winter
and cool in summer.
I am tired of owning an automobile.
I am tired of driving to places to buy things to have.
I am tired of buying things.
I am tired of buying things to use for my house.
I am tired of owning property,
of having land, of having trees and grass,
of having to drive places to buy things to use
on the grass in the summer and for the snow in the winter.
I am tired of saying, "I own this."
I am tired of saying, "This is mine."
I am tired of owning.
I don't want to own anymore.
I hope there is no such thing as a soul.
I do not want to have a soul.
If I do in fact have a soul, I want to give it away.
I would give it to the devil, if there were a devil.
I would give it away and not ask for anything in return.
I would hand it over no strings attached.
I am tired of owning things.
I am tired of having.
Here, take this.
It is the closest thing to a soul I will ever have.
Now it is yours.

Contributors

Robert Carr is the author of *Amaranth,* a chapbook scheduled for publication by Indolent Books in the spring of 2016. His poems are published or forthcoming in a variety of publications including the *The Pickled Body, The Good Men Project, Dark Matter, The Front Porch Review, Canary Literary Magazine, Bewildering Stories Magazine,* and numerous other publications. He lives in Malden, Massachusetts.

T. Crunk's first collection of poetry, *Living in the Resurrection,* was a Yale Series of Younger Poets selection. He is the author of numerous subsequent poetry collections, children's books, and works of fiction. He currently lives in Montgomery, Alabama, where he teaches creative writing in the Alabama state juvenile detention system.

Emily Dickinson "...was born in Amherst, Mass., Dec. 10, 1830, and died there May 15, 1886. Her father, Hon. Edward Dickinson, was the leading lawyer of Amherst, and was treasurer of the well-known college there situated. It was his custom once a year to hold a large reception at his house, attended by all the families connected with the institution and by the leading people of the town. On these occasions his daughter Emily emerged from her wonted retirement and did her part as gracious hostess; nor would any one have known from her manner...that this was not a daily occurrence. The annual occasion once past, she withdrew again into her seclusion, and except for a very few friends was as invisible to the world as if she had dwelt in a nunnery." (from the Preface to *Poems,* Gutenberg electronic edition)

Linda Frost is Dean of the Honors College at the University of Tennessee at Chattanooga. Her academic specialty is nineteenth century women writers. She is the author of *Never One Nation: Freaks, Savages, and Whiteness in U.S. Popular Culture, 1850-1877* and has published poetry in a variety of journals including *Witness.*

Amy Gerstler is a writer of poetry, nonfiction and journalism. *Scattered at Sea*, a book of her poems, was published by Penguin in June, 2015, and long-listed for the National Book Award. Her book *Dearest Creature* (Penguin 2009) was named a New York Times Notable Book, and was short listed for the Los Angeles Times Book Prize in Poetry. Her previous twelve books include *Ghost Girl, Medicine, Crown of*

Weeds, which won a California Book Award, *Nerve Storm,* and *Bitter Angel,* which won a National Book Critics Circle Award in poetry. She was the 2010 guest editor of the yearly anthology *Best American Poetry.* She currently teaches in the MFA Writing Program at the University of California at Irvine.

Lori Lasseter Hamilton works in a hospital as a medical records clerk by night. By day, she likes to write poetry, compete in poetry slams, and use Facebook as a diary. She earned a BA in journalism from the Univeristy of Alabama at Birmingham, with a minor in English. She currently has two chapbooks of poetry published: *live, from the emergency room* and *sawdust, soap, soil, and stars.* She has been married to Robert Hamilton for 11 years and lives in Birmingham, Alabama.

Rowan Johnson holds a doctorate from the University of Tennessee as well as an MA from the University of Nottingham, England. His work has been published in *Wordriver Literary Review, Laptop Lit Mag,* and the *Writers' Abroad Foreign Encounters Anthology.* He has also written numerous travel articles for publications such as *The Complete Woman* and *SEOUL Magazine.* Originally from South Africa, he now lives in Chattanooga, Tennessee.

Hank Lazer's nineteen books of poetry include *N24* (2014) and *N18* (2012), *Portions* (2009), and *The New Spirit* (2005). Pages from Lazer's shape-writing handwritten notebooks have been performed with soprano saxophonist Andrew Raffo Dewar in the United States and in two concerts in Havana, Cuba. Lazer's Selected Poems in translation will be appearing in books in the coming year in China, Cuba, and Italy. In 2015, Lazer was selected to receive Alabama's most prestigious literary prize, the Harper Lee Award, for lifetime achievement in literature. For more on the Notebooks, see the special online features in *Talisman #42* and *Plume #34.*

Paul Naylor's fourth full-length book of poetry, *Book of Changes,* was published by Shearsman Books in 2012. Earlier books include *Playing Well With Others* (Singing Horse Press, 2004), *Arranging Nature* (Chax Press, 2006), and *Jammed Transmission* (Tinfish Press, 2009). He is also the author of *Poetic Investigations: Singing the Holes in History* (Northwestern University Press, 1999), a study of five contemporary poets— Susan Howe, Nathaniel Mackey, Lyn Hejinian, Kamau Brathwaite, and M. Nourbese Philip.

Ted Pearson is the author of nineteen books of poetry and is a co-author of *The Grand Piano* (Mode A, 2005-2010), a ten-volume experiment in collective autobiography. His most recent books are *Extant Glyphs: 1964-1980* (Singing Horse Press, 2014), *An Intermittent Music: 1975-2010* (Chax Press, forthcoming 2016), and *The Coffin Nail Blues* (Atelos, forthcoming 2016). He lives in southern California and teaches composition at the University of Redlands.

J. R. Solonche has been publishing in magazines, journals, and anthologies since the early 70s. He is author of *Beautiful Day* (Deerbrook Editions, 2015), *Heart's Content* (Five Oaks Press, 2015), and coauthor of *Peach Girl: Poems for a Chinese Daughter* (Grayson Books, 2001).

John Stupp is the author of the 2007 Main Street Rag chapbook *The Blue Pacific* and the 2015 full-length collection *Advice from the Bed of a Friend* (also by Main Street Rag). His poetry has appeared in *The Seattle Review, Chelsea, The Pittsburgh Quarterly, 5 AM, The Pennsylvania Review, Prism International,* and other regional magazines. He has lived and worked in the Pittsburgh area for 35 years as a jazz musician, waiter, and paralegal.

Adam Vines is an assistant professor of English at the University of Alabama at Birmingham, where he is editor of *Birmingham Poetry Review*. He is the coauthor of *According to Discretion* and author of *The Coal Life*. His recent poems have appeared or are forthcoming in *Poetry, Subtropics, Green Mountains Review, The Hopkins Review,* and *Measure*.

www.ingramcontent.com/pod-product-compliance
Lightning Source LLC
Chambersburg PA
CBHW082123180726
48291CB00011B/2823